THIS

READ with ME ™

BOOK

BELONGS TO

Shannon

Library of Congress Cataloging in Publication Data

Horowitz, Susan.
   Jack and the beanstalk, with Benjy and Bubbles.

   (Read With Me series)
   SUMMARY: A rhymed retelling of the classic
tale with Benjy the bunny and Bubbles the cat
clarifying values as the story unfolds.
   [1. Stories in rhyme. 2. Fairy tales.
3. Folklore–England. 4. Giants–Fiction]
I. Razzi, James. II. Title. III. Series.
PZ8.3.H785Jac   [398.2]   [E]   77-17681
ISBN 0-03-040241-7

Jack and the Beanstalk
with Benjy and Bubbles

Adapted by SUSAN HOROWITZ
Illustrated by JIM RAZZI
Edited by RUTH LERNER PERLE

Holt, Rinehart and Winston • New York

Once, a poor little boy named Jack,
Lived with his mother in a run-down shack.
All they had was a cow so thin,
She had no milk, just bones and skin.

Mother said, "We're so poor now,
Jack, you'll have to sell our cow.
Trade her for a bag of gold,
Then come home when she is sold."

So, Jack went off to make the swap,
And right beside him, hippety-hop—
Benjy, the bunny, wiggling his tail,
Came to see the result of the sale.

Jack and his mother were poor.
He had to sell the cow.

Their journey to market just barely began,
When there, on the road, stood a strange little man.
As they went past him, Jack heard him say,
"Today, little lad, is your lucky day!
I know your cow is old and lean,
But, give her to me, and I'll give you a bean."
And Jack said, "Sir, I don't see how
One bean is worth as much as a cow."

The man said, "It's magic! I tell you no lie.
Plant this one bean; it will grow to the sky!"
"Magic!" cried Jack, "Won't Mother be proud
When she sees my beanstalk grow up through a cloud!"

Jack traded the cow for a magic bean.

Jack ran home just as fast as he could
And when he got there, his mother said, "Good!
I can see that you have sold the cow.
Give me the money. I'll count it now."
"Mother," said Jack, "just see my surprise—
A bean that will grow to a wonderful size."

"A BEAN!" cried his mother. "It's magic," said Jack.
"You fool!" cried his mother and gave him a smack.
She tossed the bean in the garden and said,
"There's no bread for supper, so just go to bed!"

Alone in his bed, Jack started to weep
And hugged Benjy tight as he went to sleep.

Jack's mother did not want a bean.
She threw it in the garden.

When Jack woke up, what did he see?
But ten times as tall as a very tall tree —
A beanstalk that grew and just didn't stop!
"Oh, Benjy!" cried Jack, "Let us climb to the top!"

So, up they both climbed, up higher than high,
Till they came to a land on top of the sky.
Not far away in that magical land
Stood a palace, all silver and golden and grand.

A tall, tall beanstalk grew in the garden.
Jack went all the way up.

A palace was at the top.
A mean Giant lived there.

Jack hurried up to the palace and knocked,
And to his surprise, the door came unlocked.
A very tall woman invited them in
And showed them the stolen treasure within.

"I'm the wife of a Giant," the woman told Jack.
"You'd better be gone before he gets back.
If he catches you here in his palace," she said,
"He'll roast you and toast you and eat you on bread!
He guards all his treasures with Bubbles, the cat,
And Bubbles means troubles—I guarantee that!"

Then all of a sudden she listened and cried,
"THE GIANT IS COMING! You'd both better hide!"

The Giant came home.
Jack hid in a bin.

Jack and Benjy both jumped in a bin
Just as the Giant and Bubbles came in.

"Fee-fi," roared the Giant, "fo-fum! What is that?"
"It's a boy and a bunny," said Bubbles, the cat.
"That's yesterday's dinner you smell," said the wife.
"It's a boy!" cried the Giant, "Bring me my knife!"

"Be calm," said the wife. "Take some gold in your lap;
Count it all up and then take a nap."
"All right," said the Giant, "bring me my gold."
So she brought him as much as two big bags would hold.
He counted it out in a great golden heap.
And Benjy and Jack never let out a peep.

Then the Giant and Bubbles both fell asleep.

The Giant counted his gold.
Then he fell asleep.

Oh, Benjy," Jack whispered, "do you think I could take
That gold for my mother before he's awake?"
"I'm sure you can do it!" said Benjy, "Just try it.
Go on your tiptoes and be very quiet."

So, up to the Giant went brave little Jack.
He scooped up the gold and tiptoed right back.
While Benjy held open the door to the bin,
Jack tossed him the gold and hurried back in.

Jack took the gold.

The Giant woke up and said, "Fee-fi-fo-fum.
Where is that boy-smell coming from?"
"What you smell," said his wife, "is some old bacon juice.
Here's something much better—your magical goose."

So the Giant just tickled the goose on the leg,
And she honked as she laid him a great golden egg.

The Giant had a magic goose.
It laid gold eggs.

"Oh, Benjy," Jack whispered, "why don't we creep
Out of the bin when the Giant's asleep?"
"As soon," Benjy said, "as his snoring is heard,
I'll grab the gold egg while you run with the bird!"

Before very long, what do you suppose?
That scary old Giant started to doze.
Then they grabbed goose and egg and managed to climb
Back in the bin in the slick nick of time!

Jack took the goose.

Then Bubbles woke up, a'meowing and hissing,
And called to the Giant, "Your treasure is missing!
There's somebody here. You'd best take a look.
Perhaps it's a boy we can bake, broil or cook!"
The Giant stood up and roared, "Fee-fi-fo-fum!
I'll find him and grind him down under my thumb!"

"What you smell," said the wife, "is an old chicken wing.
Let me bring you your magical harp that can sing."
She brought him the harp and it played such a song
That they all were asleep before very long.

The Giant had a magic harp.
It sang songs.

Then Benjy and Jack didn't wait any more,
Grabbing gold, goose and harp, they ran out the door.

The goose honked, the gold clinked, the harp sang a song
And they all reached the beanstalk before very long.

Jack took the harp and gold and goose.
He ran to the beanstalk.

As Benjy and Jack heaved a sigh of relief,
The Giant came running and roaring, "Stop, thief!"

Down the beanstalk slid Benjy and Jack
As they felt the Giant's hot breath on their back.
Down, down, down, sliding furiously fast
Till they reached the bottom and safety at last!

Jack went down the beanstalk.
The Giant went after him.

Then Jack took an ax that was lying nearby
And chopped till the beanstalk fell out of the sky.
The Giant fell down with a terrible crash
And the beanstalk caught fire and burned to an ash!

Then Benjy and Jack hurried home to their shack,
And Mother came out and hugged and kissed Jack.
"Oh, Mother!" cried Jack, "Just look what I've brought!
And I ran from the Giant and didn't get caught!
Here's a harp, and a goose and two bags of gold;
Now aren't you happy the cow has been sold?"
"I'm proud," said his mother, "of all you have done,
But mostly I'm happy to see you, dear son."

Then Jack and his mother enjoyed all the gold,
And the harp sang the story that you have been told.

Jack cut down the beanstalk.
Mother was proud of Jack.

THE END